# DREAMWORKS®

# MADAGASCAR 3

## ON THE RUN!

by Pamela Bobowicz

MADAGASCAR 3: ON THE RUN!
A BANTAM BOOK 978 0 857 51092 1

First published in Great Britain by Bantam,
an imprint of Random House Children's Books
A Random House Group Company.

This edition published 2012

1 3 5 7 9 10 8 6 4 2

Madagascar 3 © 2012 DreamWorks Animation L.L.C.

The Random House Group Limited supports The Forest Stewardship Council (FSC®),
the leading international forest certification organization. Our books carrying the FSC label
are printed on FSC®-certified paper. FSC is the only forest certification scheme endorsed by the
leading environmental organizations, including Greenpeace. Our paper procurement policy
can be found at www.randomhouse.co.uk/environment

MIX
Paper from
responsible sources
FSC® C020056

Bantam Books are published by Random House Children's Books,
61–63 Uxbridge Road, London W5 5SA

www.**kids**at**randomhouse**.co.uk
www.**totallyrandombooks**.co.uk
www.**randomhouse**.co.uk

Addresses for companies within The Random House Group Limited can be found at:
www.randomhouse.co.uk/offices.htm

THE RANDOM HOUSE GROUP Limited Reg. No. 954009

A CIP catalogue record for this book is available from the British Library.

Printed in China

Alex, Marty, Gloria and Melman had been away from New York for a long time. On Alex's birthday, he wished that they could all go home.

"Well then, let's go!" Marty said.

"We can't go home without the Penguins," Gloria pointed out.

"We should go to Monte Carlo and get them ourselves," Alex said.

So the group set off straight away.

In a Monte Carlo hotel, the
Penguins were having a great time.
They were currently working on a new
training technique: pillow fighting.

"Ha! You pillow fight like a bunch
of little girls," Skipper challenged
his men.

He didn't see Rico sneak up behind him. *Poof!* There was an explosion of feathers, as Rico's pillow crashed down over the Penguins' leader.

"Chimichanga!" Skipper cried in horror. "These pillows are filled with baby birds!"

Meanwhile, four heads popped
up out of the Mediterranean Sea: a
hippo, a zebra, a lion and a giraffe.

"There it is," Melman mumbled
around the mouthpiece of his
snorkel. "The casino."

"Perfect," Alex replied. "That's where we'll find the Penguins."

As the four animals swam towards the casino, King Julien followed with Mort and Maurice. Fireworks from the boat announced his arrival.

Inside the casino, the Penguins and the Chimps had dressed up as the King of Versailles using white face paint, a wig and bright red lipstick. They were playing roulette and winning big!

Suddenly, the Zoosters crashed into the casino. People screamed in fear and ran, as the animals tried to escape.

The casino guards called Animal Control Officer Capitain Chantel Dubois. She snapped on her gloves and set off after the animals.

As the guards gave chase, a black
armoured van rolled up. The animals
climbed in.

Skipper buckled himself in at
the controls. "Step on it, boys!" he
commanded.

The animals sped through the streets of Monte Carlo. Melman stuck his head out of the window, on the lookout for Capitain Dubois and her team.

"Wahoo!" he cried as his ears flapped in the wind.

But Captain Dubois spotted
Melman and so her team raced after
the van.

King Julien thought the flashing
lights were paparazzi looking for him.
He opened the back door. "Don't take
any photos," he said, striking a pose.

Suddenly, he was hit with a dart. He
collapsed onto the floor. The other
animals quickly closed the door.

While the Lemurs checked on King Julien, the Penguins prepared for the next part of the plan. The animals were supposed to meet the Chimps to catch an escape plane.

"ETA to rendezvous point?" Skipper cried.

"Two minutes, thirty-seven seconds, sir!" Kowalski said.

Maurice looked out of the back window. Capitain Dubois and her team were still hot on their trail. Would they make it to the plane?

"The crazy woman is catching up!" he warned. The Penguins had to work faster!

"We need more power!" Skipper said. "Time to fire up Kowalski's nuclear reactor."

He pushed a button and the floor

panels slid away. Skipper switched on the reactor and it began to glow.

The van surged forwards and then crashed into the edge of a building.

Just then, the Chimps arrived with their Super-Plane! The Penguins boarded the plane and shot bananas at Capitain Dubois, as the Zoosters made it to safety.

The animals' good luck ran out quickly, though.

"The gear assembly is badly damaged," Kowalski told Skipper. "It's only a matter of time before . . ."

*CRASH!*

The plane crash-landed.

The animals pulled themselves out of the wreckage.

"The plane's wrecked. Never to fly again," Skipper said.

"We're not going home," Alex said sadly as he looked at his friends. "We're *never* going home."

Suddenly, they heard police sirens in the distance. Capitain Dubois! They had to hide.

The animals looked around. Alex spotted a circus train. They couldn't blend in at a casino, but maybe they could at a circus . . .

Alex banged on the door. "Hey!" he called.

The door slid open and a scary, growling tiger leaned out.

The animals jumped back in surprise.

"Please," Alex said to the tiger.

"You've got to hide us."

But the tiger shook his head.

"Absolutely no outsiders. This train is for circus animals only."

The tiger slammed the door. The
Zoosters were desperate.

Alex heard the circus animals
arguing inside.

"If they are in trouble, we cannot
leave them out there," a voice said.

The train started moving. Thinking quickly, Alex called out, "Wait! We *are* circus animals!"

Melman, Marty and Gloria piped up, too. "Circus is my life!" they each shouted.

The door opened and the tiger was joined by a jaguar and a sea lion.

"They are circus," the jaguar said.
"Circus animals stick together."

The Zoosters hurried onboard and closed the door, just as police torches lit up the train.

Once again, the animals thought they were safe. But the tiger, Vitaly, told them that the Circus Master didn't allow stowaways on his train.

That's when Skipper had an idea. "The circus owner may allow stowaways . . . if the stowaways just happen to be the owners."

Dressed as the King of Versailles again, the Penguins and the Chimps made an offer for the circus. Phil stared down at the owner – he really wanted to win this deal.

The Circus Master's eyes went wide
at the sight of the Chimps' pile of
jewels and gold.

As the clowns giggled greedily behind him, the Circus Master brought out the circus deeds.

"You have a deal, *mi amigo*," he said with a smile.

As quickly as they could, the Circus
Master and clowns packed up their
car and piled in.

"I am sure this circus will bring
you great success!" the Circus Master
said. He gave the King a big smile.
"Well, I guess this is goodbye.
And good luck!"

The clowns burst into laughter as the Circus Master drove away.

Phil held out the deeds to show the other animals.

They'd done it! They'd bought the circus from the owner and now they could stay safely onboard.

Alex, Gloria, Marty and Melman smiled.

"There's nothing left for us to do but ride this circus train all the way to New York City," Alex said.

The Penguins took the controls as the other animals settled in. They were going home at last!